BEASTS
—OF—
OLYMPUS

To Al and Ray Preston,
Thank you so much for helping this to happen.
I know the kids will be thrilled.
All best, Lucy

For Finnegan, who reminds me to believe
that anything is possible—BB

PENGUIN WORKSHOP
Penguin Young Readers Group
An Imprint of Penguin Random House LLC

Text copyright © 2018 by Lucy Coats. Illustrations copyright © 2018 by Brett Bean. All rights reserved.
Published by Penguin Workshop, an imprint of Penguin Random House LLC, 345 Hudson Street,
New York, New York 10014. PENGUIN and PENGUIN WORKSHOP are trademarks of Penguin Books Ltd,
and the W colophon is a trademark of Penguin Random House LLC. Printed in the USA.

Library of Congress Cataloging-in-Publication Data is available.

ISBN 9780515159523   10 9 8 7 6 5 4 3 2 1

BEASTS
–OF–
OLYMPUS

by Lucy Coats   art by Brett Bean

The Unicorn Emergency

PENGUIN WORKSHOP
An Imprint of Penguin Random House

CHAPTER 1

FAREWELL TO ASGARD

Demon cracked one eye open, groaned, and shut it again. His brain felt as if Hephaestus had been hitting it with hammers, and there was a strange ringing in his ears. It had been a very late night.

"Go 'way!" he said as a hand shook his shoulder roughly. "It's too early."

"No it's not," said Thrud Thorsdaughter, his new friend and the latest shield-maiden of Asgard. "You've been asleep for ages. I haven't even been to bed yet," she added proudly.

Demon groaned again. The evening before was all a bit of a blur. There'd been a lot of very loud singing with Thrud's fellow maidens, and once most of the gods had left, there had also been a great deal of toasting his new status as holder of the Order of Yggdrasil. The Valkyries had insisted he try several sips of their mead, which had made his head go all funny and his knees wobble like a newborn lamb's. He seemed to remember some rather energetic dancing, too. Sitting up cautiously, he opened his other eye.

"Tell me I didn't make a complete fool of myself last night," he said. Thrud sniggered and hurriedly turned it into a cough.

"Let's just say that your version of the Bear Dance will go down in Asgard history, but your song about Fenrir needs some work on the wolf howling," she said. "Come on, you'll feel better after breakfast."

The feasting hall of Valhalla was strewn with gnawed bones, overturned tables, empty mead flagons—and quite a few snoring bodies. The Asgardians definitely partied hard.

"I'm not really sure I feel much like breakfast," Demon said, avoiding a puddle of something questionable on the floor. "I think I'll go and check on Goldbristle instead." Goldbristle was the boar he'd cured the day before, banishing the darkness caused by Loki, Thrud's evil uncle.

"Oh, he's long gone," said Thrud, skipping toward the doors and flinging them wide open, so that the diamond-bright light of day filled the hall. "Frey couldn't wait to drive up into the sky with him this morning. Doesn't it all look WONDERFUL?" she exclaimed.

Demon blinked and screwed up his eyes, trying hard to ignore the sensation of daggers being driven into his skull as a million rainbow reflections bounced off the snow-covered streets.

"Lovely," he muttered, putting his furry sheepskin hood up to block out the rays. Just then, a huge golden-haired god carrying a gigantic silver hammer came striding into view. It was Thor, god of thunder.

"Dad!" Thrud yelled, running out of the door and leaping into his arms.

"How's my little shield-maiden?" Thor asked, whirling her around. "Have you tried out Mjolnirina yet?"

Thrud shook her head, stroking the small silver hammer hanging at her belt.

"Not yet," she said. "I wanted to see if she could beat your Mjolnir. Let's put them through their paces." She turned and beckoned to Demon. "Come on, Olympus Boy. You can watch."

As she and Thor strode off down the snowy streets, Demon stumbled after them. His head now felt as if it were full of mush. These Asgardians were very strange. How could Thrud and Thor talk about their hammers as if they were alive?

He soon found out. The minute they reached the other side of Asgard's high wall, Thrud and Thor began whirling Mjolnirina and Mjolnir around their heads.

"Whee!" yelled Thrud, letting go.

"Woo-hooo!" shouted Thor, launching Mjolnir upward at exactly the same moment. Demon's eyes nearly fell out of his head. Instead of rising and then falling to the ground, the two hammers shot up and up into the sky. When they were no more than dark specks against the blue, white clouds boiled up around them. Thunder roared above, and then, like two streaks of silver lightning, the hammers returned to earth, hitting with a ground-shaking thump. Where they landed, the snow began to steam and hiss.

Thor held out his hand.

"Come, Mjolnir!" he roared, and the huge hammer heaved itself out of the earth and returned to his hand.

Demon blinked. It was definitely as if the thing was alive and could understand.

"Come, Mjolnirina!" Thrud called.

Nothing happened.

"Mjolnirina, COME!" she called again. There was a sort of wet hiccup, and the little hammer flipped and flopped its way to her over the snow, falling at her feet.

"Hmm," said Thor. "You may have to work on the obedience commands a bit. But good first effort." He grinned at Demon, showing very white teeth under a magnificent mustache. "Perhaps you have a potion for your head, young Pandemonius?"

Demon grinned back, his headache finally
lifting. It was hard to be formal with a god like Thor.

"Not me, Your Humungous Hammeriness," he
said. "My potions are strictly for sick beasts."

Thor clapped him on the shoulder, sending him
flying into a nearby snowbank.

"By Odin's hat," the big god said, fetching Demon
out with one meaty hand and dusting the ice off him
clumsily. "I forgot my own strength again."

"That reminds me. I went to check on Fenrir this morning. He's still asleep, but he does seem to be whimpering a lot."

Immediately, Demon felt guilty. The day before, he'd put the enormous wolf into a permanent sleep to stop him from killing Odin, the king of the Asgardians. Fenrir's wolf mind was truly and properly lost to madness, but Demon still felt bad that he hadn't been able to cure him.

"Maybe he's having nightmares," said Thrud. "I don't suppose you can do much about those."

"Nightmares are terrible things," said Thor. "I have them myself." He shuddered. "Dreamed I was being eaten by old Fafnir the dragon once, teeth crunching, flesh tearing and all. Took me days to shake it off. Even Odin admitted that was a bad one when I told it to him."

"I might be able to do something," Demon said slowly as they walked back into Asgard again. "But it would have to wait till I get back to Olympus. There's somebody there who is a specialist in dreams. His name is Morpheus."

"Would he come here, then?" Thrud asked. Demon nodded.

"I think so. He helped me once before, when I had some mad horses to manage."

"Mad horses?" Thor asked. "That sounds like a good adventure. Tell us more."

So Demon told them about the mad meat-eating mares that horrible Heracles had left in his mom's village, and how Morpheus had given them permanent dreams of hay and peace.

"Sounds like just the god we need here," said Thor. "Fenrir will be dreaming of chasing fluffy bunnies in no time."

Just then, Demon saw a tall, curvy figure up ahead, wrapped in white furs. All around her the ice flowed into curving tendrils, which exploded into bouquets of exquisite ice blossoms. It was Demeter, goddess of fruitfulness.

"Ah, there you are, Pandemonius," she said as she reached them. "My work here is done, now that Goldbristle is back in the sky. The apple trees are all back in fruit, and it's time we returned to Olympus. Gather your things and meet me at Heimdall's Gate. Hurry now."

Demon bowed.

"Yes, Your Fabulous Fruitiness," he said. "Right away." The Olympian gods were much more formal than the Asgardian ones, and he didn't want to take the chance of being turned into a giant peach or something worse.

Once he'd gathered up his magic medicine box and stowed Far Caller, the little horn Odin had given him, in his bundle, Thrud led him to Heimdall's Gate, where Demeter was already waiting.

"I'll miss you," said Thrud, giving him a hug. "Come back soon!"

Demon hugged her back.

"Or you could come visit Olympus," he said with an exaggerated shiver. "We have proper sunshine there—none of this freezy snow stuff!" Thrud only laughed.

Demon looked around as he joined Demeter, expecting the cloud ship he'd arrived on. But there was nothing visible. How were they going to return to Olympus?

Just then, Heimdall arrived. The herald of Asgard's white beard was plaited into three jutting forks, each with small icicles hanging from it. His eyes were still the pale white-blue of an early winter sky.

"Ready?" he boomed.

Demeter nodded, gesturing for Demon to stand beside her.

Heimdall took the golden horn that twisted
around his body like a huge snake and blew it softly.

The sound Demon heard was like a crisp dip in a cold forest pool. All the hair on his body lifted as a rainbow bridge spun forward out of nothing, filling the sky with color.

"Step forward onto Bifrost, and state your destination," the god commanded.

Demeter walked confidently onto the rainbow, beckoning Demon to stand beside her with one imperious finger.

"Olympus!" she cried.

It was not at all like traveling on the Iris Express. Bifrost was more like a moving road. Demon tried not to look down at the earth, so far below, as they sped forward. The icy wind whipped his hair around his cheeks, blowing his hood off, and he clutched his coat around him.

Gradually, though, the air got warmer and warmer, and by the time they approached Olympus, he was becoming uncomfortably hot.

"Phew!" said Demeter, making a very un-goddess-like flapping gesture with her hand as she stepped off. At once, all her furs disappeared, leaving her in her usual white goddess robes as she vanished with a sparkle of lights and a delicious smell of ripe orchards.

"Not a word of thanks, as usual," said a gruff voice. "Typical goddess."

"Um, thank you for getting me back home safely," Demon said, trying to shed his woolly coat and boots.

"My pleasure," said Bifrost, just as a familiar flurry of colors arched down out of the evening sky.

"And just who is THIS intruder?" purred Iris the rainbow goddess dangerously, twining herself around the bridge.

"Iris, meet Bifrost; Bifrost, meet Iris," said Demon, deciding to leave undressing till later. There had been a distinct edge to Iris's voice—one he knew all too well.

"I'll, er, just leave you two to it, shall I?" he said, hurrying off in the direction of the Stables of the Gods. He knew a goddess in a temper when he heard one, and it was always best to move far, far away for fear of being turned into something unnatural.

CHAPTER 2

STAR NYMPHS, AHOY!

The Stables were quiet as he approached, panting. The sooner he got rid of the rest of his furry Asgard clothes and put on something normal, the better.

"Hey, Pan's scrawny kid," said the griffin, flying down off its perch on the roof. "How was the frozen North? Did you bring me back a nice big reindeer leg to chew on?"

"Unfortunately not," said Demon. "But I did have an adventure with some dark elves and a very scary dragon. I'll tell you all about it as soon as I've got out of all these hot clothes."

The griffin cocked its head sideways, looking at him out of one orange eye.

"Your face does look a bit like the red part of old Heffy's forge," it said. "All glowing and shiny."

Demon rolled his eyes.

"Thanks for the compliment," he said.

Quickly, he dumped everything and ran up the stairs to the loft above the Stables where he slept. It was a big relief to put on his tunic and feel cool again. When he got back down, his assistant, Bion the faun, was there, fending off the griffin, who was pecking at his small hooves.

"Leave Bion alone," Demon said. "You know he doesn't like you doing that."

By the time he had inspected the Stables and told Bion and the griffin all about his adventures, he was yawning. His late night with the Valkyries was definitely catching up with him.

"I'm going to turn in," he said. "I'll leave you to do the last checks, Bion."

"Sweet dreams," said the griffin.

Demon stopped dead. How could he have forgotten? He'd promised to send Morpheus to Asgard. But how was he to get hold of the god of dreams? Suddenly, he remembered. Morpheus had given him a dream catcher. Maybe he could contact him through that. Fumbling right at the bottom of his pouch, his fingers touched something curiously squishy. He pulled out a shiny black crystal, whose edges seemed to blur and shift. Clutching it in his hand, he climbed up to the loft and fell into bed, snuggling down under his familiar spider-silk blanket as he stared into the dream catcher's depths. The rainbows swirling within it were . . . so . . . soothing . . .

"Please, Morpheus, help Fenrir," he whispered as his eyelids drooped shut.

Almost immediately, or so it seemed, he found himself floating in a gray place, with myriad silver stars whirling in a night sky that shimmered and changed in dizzying swirls. Black sand stretched as far as his eyes could see, and on the horizon there were two huge arches, one bone white, one a golden brown. Suddenly, a shadowy dot appeared through the white arch, very far away but rapidly coming closer, resolving itself into a strange being, all long thin arms and legs, and eyes like pools of deep water. In its hand it carried a torch of black-and-gold flame.

"Pandemonius!" said the god, sounding

surprised. "How did you get here?"

Quickly, Demon explained what he'd done. Then he told Morpheus about Fenrir.

"I think he's having terrible nightmares," he finished, "and you were the only person I could think of who might be able to help."

"Very well," said Morpheus. "But don't use the dream catcher in that way again. This is a dangerous place to be. Anything you think here can become real." He made a twisty gesture with his torch, and Demon knew nothing more till he woke the next morning. On the floor by his bed, written in flowing letters of black sand, was a message.

The Wolf dreams well now . . . M.

Demon was just pouring a big load of Sun Cow poo down the poo chute, to the appreciative roars of the hundred-armed monsters beneath, when the griffin landed beside him in a flurry of golden feathers.

"Hey, Pan's scrawny kid, old Heffy wants to see you immediately. I should run if I were you. He sounded quite bothered."

Demon left his wheelbarrow tipped on its side and started to run up the rocky mountain path to Hephaestus's forge at once. He had a bad feeling right down to his toes. Heffy didn't usually get bothered—he was quite calm for a god, really. What could have gone wrong? Had the Colchian Dragon eaten something that made it gassy again? Was the whole of Olympus about to blow up?

Puffing and panting, he hurtled into the forge to find the blacksmith god kneeling in front of a large flashing red gemstone set into the wall, which was making a horrible wailing sound. The Colchian Dragon was curled into a large purple ball with its tail wrapped around its head.

"What's THAT?" Demon shouted, putting his fingers in his ears.

"The Typhon alarm," Hephaestus yelled back. "I'm trying to turn it off!" He raised a huge, grimy fist and gave it a wallop. Suddenly, there was a blissful quiet, although the jewel was still flashing red.

"Who's Typhon?" Demon asked into the silence as the Colchian Dragon uncurled itself with a rattle of scales.

Hephaestus sighed, tugging on his beard.

"He's a terrible hundred-headed monster," said the smith god. "Zeus put me in charge of him. He's been asleep under a mountain for the last thousand years, but that alarm tells me he's waking up for some reason. I need to go and see what's up, and you're coming with me, Pandemonius. Every one of his heads is some sort of animal—bears, lions, dragons, that sort of thing—so I've a feeling we'll need those pipes of yours."

"Can I come, too?" asked the Colchian Dragon. "I haven't been out for ages, and I've cried out LOTS of fire jewels for you." It looked sideways at Demon. "And I helped you with your display for the gods of the North, too," it said.

"Oh, very well," said Hephaestus. "But we'll have to borrow Helios's sun boat. You're too big to fit in the Iris Express now."

A short while later, Demon, Hephaestus, and the dragon were installed in a huge golden boat, round as a bowl, with a big oar at the back. Demon had his medicine bag, his pipes, and four enormous bags of charcoal for the dragon in case it got hungry.

"Now," said the smith god, "let's see if I remember how this thing works." He wiggled the oar left, then right, and with a jerk, the sun boat shot up into the sky. Higher and higher they went, until the air turned cold and dark as the boat lurched from side to side, banging into stars along the way.

"By Zeus's ears," said Hephaestus, wrestling with the oar, which seemed to have a mind of its own, "I think this wretched contraption needs a steering modification."

Tiny chips of bright silver stardust clinked and tinkled as they fell into the boat, flickering out and turning black. The dragon nibbled on them.

"Tasty!" it said. "Like charcoal but with a hint of sky."

Clinging to the side to keep from being thrown out, Demon scooped some of the stardust into a wide-necked bottle. He'd show it to Chiron, his centaur teacher, and find out if it could be used as medicine, he thought. But before the bottle was more than half-full, Hephaestus gave a yell, wrenching the oar over to his right.

"Star nymphs, ahoy!" he shouted. "Watch out! Boat coming through!" Suddenly, there was a tremendous bang, and all at once the sun boat was full of thrashing limbs, angry screams, and the faint smell of deep cold, tinged with flowers.

"Oof!" said Demon as someone landed on him, knocking him backward into the Colchian Dragon, which roared angrily and let out a belch of purple flame. Everything was chaos for a few minutes as the boat veered and rocked, nearly tipping over. Eventually Hephaestus got it back under control, and as it resumed its progress through the sky, Demon saw that the limbs and the angry screams belonged to six nymphs, their floaty robes silver against the gold of the boat. Each had a crown of living stars whirling around her head, and they shone so brightly that Demon had to squint to see them properly. The smallest of them was standing in front of Hephaestus, shaking one long finger at him.

"Careless, clumsy oaf of a god!" she shrieked. "Take us back at once! How dare you kidnap us like this?"

Hephaestus looked embarrassed.

"Now, now, Maia," he said. "It was an accident. This wretched sun boat of Helios's isn't easy to steer, you know . . ."

"She always gets so angry," said a voice in Demon's ear. It was the nymph who had fallen on him. "I'm Alcyone, by the way. One of the seven Pleiades, you know. Sorry if I squashed you."

"Nice to meet you," said Demon. "I'm Demon." Then he frowned, counting noses. "But there are only six of you."

Alcyone laughed.

"Oh, Electra's invisible. She'll be around here somewhere, but she's rather shy." Her eyes twinkled. "She's looking at you right now. I think she might like you."

Demon blushed. He wasn't at all sure about an invisible nymph admirer.

CHAPTER 3

TERRIBLE TYPHON

The rest of the journey was taken up by quite a lot of arguing, and more shouting, as each of the visible Pleiades in turn tried to persuade Hephaestus to turn back. Demon spent the time trying to calm down the Colchian Dragon.

"This was supposed to be a nice treat," it moaned. "All this aggravation can't be good for my digestion. I'll turn red, and it'll all start again—you see if it doesn't. I'm sure I can feel the gas building up now."

"You won't turn red, and I'm sure your stomach will be fine," Demon said soothingly. "Have some of this nice charcoal, and then you can clean up the stardust so nobody slips on it." He tipped half a sack of charcoal down the dragon's throat, and soon it was munching and mumbling contentedly. It was a beast of simple needs.

"BE QUIET, ALL OF YOU!" Hephaestus roared finally. "OR I'LL SEND YOU TO APHRODITE!"

There was a small silence.

"Oh, please don't," said Alcyone. "You know how we hate being her nymphs-in-waiting. She's so very . . . well . . . pink and fluffy. But we really do need to be back in our part of the sky soon, or everything will get in a terrible muddle. The stars do wander so, and if we're not there to herd them back into place, all the earth humans in their ships will get terribly confused."

"Where are we going, anyway?" Maia butted in.

By the time Hephaestus had explained about the Typhon alarm, the boat was swooping low over the sea. Beneath them lay a large island, shaped like a strange dog's head, with a mountain just where the dog's ear would be. Large boulders flew up into the air around the mountain, raining down onto the ground, which shook with the impact. There was a huge hole in the top, which seemed to be getting bigger as they watched. The mountain was also roaring, so loudly that even with his fingers in his ears, Demon could feel the sound through his whole body, as if it were being buffeted by an enormous wind. He saw Hephaestus's mouth move but couldn't tell what he was saying.

"Take us out of range!" Demon yelled, but he couldn't even hear his own words, so he pointed upward instead, hoping Heffy would understand. Immediately, the sun boat swooped toward the heavens again, leaving the dreadful racket behind.

"Well," said the smith god, "I think it's safe to say Typhon's awake. But how are we going to put him back to sleep? He'll never hear those pipes of yours, Pandemonius." He turned to the star nymphs.

"You nymphs sing, don't you?"

Maia nodded.

"Well, yes," she said. "We sing to soothe the stars when they get upset. But I don't see how—"

"Sing, then," Hephaestus commanded her. "Sing for all you're worth." And he turned the boat downward again.

It wasn't so much a song, Demon thought as the

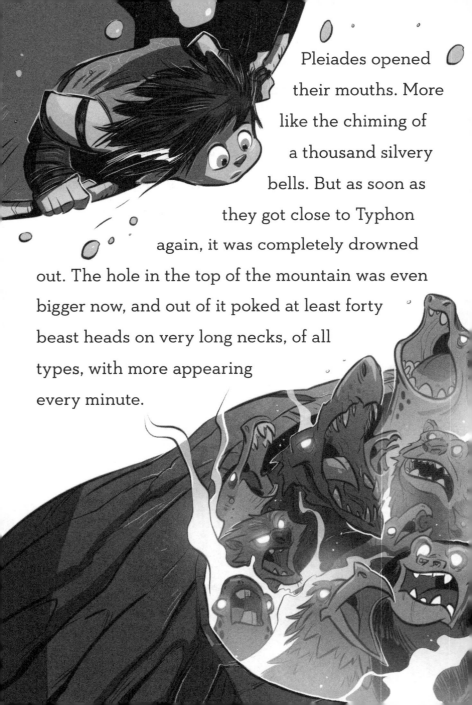

Pleiades opened their mouths. More like the chiming of a thousand silvery bells. But as soon as they got close to Typhon again, it was completely drowned out. The hole in the top of the mountain was even bigger now, and out of it poked at least forty beast heads on very long necks, of all types, with more appearing every minute.

Each head was a hundred times the size of the actual animal, and each was clearly furious. Hephaestus steered the boat upward again hurriedly, as several of the heads lunged at them.

"He's nearly free!" the god yelled when they could hear again. "We have to do something fast! Zeus will be furious if he escapes!"

Demon shuddered. He didn't want to be anywhere near a furious Zeus.

"But what?" he shouted back. Then his eyes fell on the Colchian Dragon. The beast was curled into a shivering ball, and the back half of it had turned bright red with fear. An idea flicked into his mind. It was a very dangerous idea, but it was the only thing he could come up with.

"Do you think a dragon fart might stun Typhon long enough for me to play my pipes?" he asked slowly.

Hephaestus's mouth fell open, and the Pleiades

all let out tiny shrieks of horror.

"Noooo!" moaned the dragon. "Don't make me. Mustkeepitinmustkeepitinmustkeepitin!"

Demon stroked its purple head gently.

"Just the one," he said. "I promise you can have all the charcoal right afterward to turn you purple again. And I'll never ever ask you to do it again."

Hephaestus scratched his head with one grimy finger.

"I don't know, young Pandemonius," he said. "It's very risky. What if there's a spark from somewhere? It could blow us all to kingdom come."

"And think of the smell!" all the star nymphs chorused, holding their noses.

"Oh, the shame, the terrible shame!" the dragon groaned, curling itself into an even smaller ball of red and purple misery.

Demon scrambled to his feet, making the boat rock.

"If we don't do something soon, Typhon will be free, and I for one don't want to face Zeus's wrath. Do you?" he asked.

Hephaestus glared at him, but Demon didn't back down, and after a short pause, they all shook their heads, even the dragon.

"All right, then," Demon said, delving into his medicine bag. "Let's do this. Luckily, I've got a whole bunch of Chiron's special masks in here. Put them on."

"Ordering me about," Hephaestus grumbled as he fitted the mask of cotton and reeds to his hairy face with one hand. "Those gods of the North gave you too much freedom, I reckon. What happened to all those nice manners?"

Down they went again into the maelstrom of noise. Demon helped the dragon to position its bottom over the edge of the boat, draping its tail out of

the way, and as Hephaestus steered as close as
he could to Typhon's gnashing, roaring heads, the
dragon squeezed its eyes shut,
aimed, and let out
an enormous
blast of gas.

Immediately, the heads were shrouded in a hazy
cloud of noxious green. Shortly afterward, the roars
turned to choking and then fell silent. Zooming
even closer, Hephaestus took the boat down to
hover just above the huge hole in the mountain.
Through the haze they could see Typhon's many
heads slumped on the edge. Demon spotted every
animal he knew, and some he didn't.

"Mmphrm pmphrm?" Hephaestus asked, his

voice muffled by the mask. Demon turned from helping the dragon down.

"Whmph?" he said as he poured three bags of charcoal down its eager throat, avoiding the very sharp rows of teeth. The star nymphs were all fanning the green smoke away with little moans of dismay.

The smith god pointed urgently to where Demon's pipes stuck out of his tunic, and then to where one of Typhon's heads was beginning to stir. Demon pulled them out, about to put them to his lips, when he realized the problem. How was he going to play them with his mask on? The smith god must have realized at the same time. Reaching down, he picked up one of the charcoal bags and began to flap it very fast. The green haze around the boat disappeared, just as Demon heard a small roar from below, and then another. He'd have to risk it. If Typhon woke up, all the dragon's work would have been for nothing.

Taking a deep breath, he ripped off the mask and put the pipes to his lips, blowing Pan's special twiddle notes. The roars stopped immediately, and as he peered over the edge of the sun boat, all of Typhon's heads, eyes closed and sleeping, slithered back down into the ground and disappeared.

The dragon hiccupped. One tiny purple-blue spark floated over the side of the boat, and then downward. With a different kind of roar, the green gas below them exploded, sending the boat spiraling upward, rocking from side to side and spinning out of control. Underneath, the hole in the top of the mountain fell in on itself, boulders bouncing and bounding down the sides, until all that was left was a small round depression in the ground.

Hephaestus wrestled with the steering oar, and eventually the sun boat was back under his control.

Though everyone was tumbled and mussed and bruised, they all cheered as they sped high over the sea and away from Typhon's lair.

"Well done, Dragon," said Demon as it munched on its charcoal, slowly turning purple again.

"Double-extra rations for you when we get back," said Hephaestus, grinning, as the star nymphs crowded around it, patting its scaly flanks.

CHAPTER 4

NOTE FROM NOWHERE

"Whoa!" said the smith god suddenly, pointing downward. "What's that? I'm sure it wasn't here when I came by before." Demon and the star nymphs rushed to the side of the sun boat, making it tip dangerously.

Two enormous pillars of rock loomed up out of the land beneath, one on either side of the sea. Clouds of gray dust hung about them as they shifted and settled, rumbling slightly.

"I don't remember seeing them before, either,"

said Maia. "How could they have got there?"

"I don't know," Hephaestus said slowly. "But you can be sure I'll make it my business to find out. I think we found out where the disturbance that woke Typhon up came from."

"Look!" said Alcyone softly, poking him in the ribs as they flew past. At first Demon couldn't see anything, but then he noticed a tiny figure striding away southward from the mess. It was a figure he thought he recognized, though he'd only seen it once before, in the desert near the Mountains of Burning Sand.

"Horrible Heracles," he muttered. "I bet you he caused all this." He was about to tell Hephaestus, when all the star nymphs screamed.

"Oh no!" Maia yelled, looking up into the heavens. "I KNEW this would happen. All the stars are wandering. Take us back quick, Hephaestus." Demon felt a brush of something against his back as he stared upward at the jumble of stars, and then the Pleiades all started to sing. Louder and louder their silvery voices got as they headed into the emptiness of the heavens, and he sat down, leaning against the warm bulk of the dragon again, and drifted off to sleep listening to their soothing melody.

A long time later, he woke to a rough hand shaking his shoulder.

"Out you get, young Pandemonius," Hephaestus said. "We're home, and I have to clean this boat out before I return it to Helios. Stardust and charcoal are all over."

"I'll help," Demon mumbled, but Hephaestus shook his head.

"The Colchian Dragon and I will do it," he said. "It's all purple and perky now. You get off to bed. You've got a lot of poo shoveling to do tomorrow,

I expect." He ruffled Demon's hair. "And find your manners again, young Stable Master. If you try ordering the other gods about like you did me today, you'll find yourself turned into a fried sardine, I shouldn't wonder."

As Demon stumbled sleepily down the mountain toward the Stables, he couldn't help wishing for a bit of peace. He'd had a lot of adventures lately, and all he wanted was to spend some time quietly with his beasts.

"And I've got homework from Chiron to catch up on, too," he grumbled to himself. Chiron was his centaur teacher who lived down on earth, in a cave on Mount Pelion, and was also the greatest healer who'd ever lived. Climbing slowly up to his loft, Demon was just about to fall into bed and go to sleep again, when he saw a bit of paper lying on his bed. It was very mangled around the edges, with strange, uneven holes on one side. When he picked it up, it was also sticky, as if somebody or something had drooled on it.

"What in the name of Zeus's big toenail . . . ?" he said, picking it up and opening it.

COME QUICKLY! UNICORN EMERGENCY! it said in glowing green-gold letters.

Wiping his damp hand on his tunic, he went over to Bion's side of the loft and shook him awake.

"What's this?" he asked the bleary-eyed faun. "Where did it come from, and who's it from?"

Bion shook his head, yawning.

"Dunno," he said. "It was here when I came to bed. Nobody came to the Stables to deliver it."

Demon ran down the stairs again, wide awake now. He rushed over to the unicorn's stall at the far end, but she was curled up and fast asleep, tiny, whiffling snores coming from her nostrils. Opening the door very gently, he tiptoed in, careful not to wake her. Unicorns didn't really like boys very much, so normally the nymphs looked after her and milked her when Aphrodite needed her weekly bath. Unicorn milk was very good for beautiful skin, according to the goddess. Holding his breath, he checked her shining horn and flanks and legs for damage, but he could see nothing that was in any way an emergency. Backing away carefully, he felt for the door behind him. A large splinter ran into his thumb.

"Ouch!" he said, without thinking. The unicorn's eyes, blue as a summer sky, flicked open.

"Aargh!" she scream-whinnied. "A boy-hoy-hoy in my stable! A nasty, dirty boy-hoy-hoy!" Scrambling to her feet and lowering her horn, she charged. Demon whipped around and ran, slamming the door shut behind him. The horn came through the bars, scraping hard along the side of his scalp.

It hurt. A lot. And what felt like a whole river of blood was now running down beside his ear. Immediately, Offy and Yukus, the two magical healing snakes who lived around his neck as a golden necklace, flashed into action, mending the wound.

"Thanks, boys," he said shakily once he had retreated to a safe distance.

"It wasss our pleasure," said the snakes, settling back around his neck again.

Demon sat down on a bale of sun hay to recover. Suddenly, there was a rustle nearby and the scent of something he thought he recognized. The hairs on the back of his neck prickled, as if someone was watching him.

"Is anyone there?" he called. But there was no reply.

"What's up, Pan's scrawny kid?" asked a sleepy griffin voice. "What are you making such a racket for? You're ruining my beauty sleep."

"Never mind," Demon said, as he climbed back up to the loft. "Go back to sleep. It'll keep till morning."

He didn't sleep very well. Nightmares of unicorns with broken legs, unicorns with purple spots, and worst of all, unicorn skeletons kept waking him up. As Eos drew back the pink curtains of dawn, he jumped out of bed and grabbed the note, stuffing it inside his tunic. Until he knew who had sent it, he couldn't do much about it, though, and it was bothering him. The thought of any animal in pain was not something he was ever happy about.

The Stables below were full of the noise of waking beasts, yawning, stretching, and in some cases clamoring for their morning ambrosia cake. Doris the Hydra was particularly affectionate, drooling mightily and rubbing its nine heads against him as the buckets of food were tipped into its manger. Behind him came Bion with the poo barrow and shovel, and between them they had the Stables spick-and-span in almost no time at all.

"All right!" said Demon when they were finished. "Listen up, everybody. Did anyone come with a note for me yesterday?"

Anyone else would have heard a whole lot of

animal noises. But Demon could speak every beast language. All he heard was a whole lot of NO. He didn't think he'd better go near the unicorn again, so he stepped outside and had a word with his friend, the nymph Althea.

"Can you ask the unicorn if she knows anything about this, please?" he asked her, showing her the note. Her nose wrinkled as she touched it.

"Ugh! All slobbery," she said. "And who writes in glowy ink now? That's so last year." But she agreed to ask. When she came back, she was shaking her head.

"The unicorn doesn't know anything about it. She hasn't seen her family for years, so now she's very worried. Oh, and she said to tell you to have a bath. You stink of poo!" With that, she ran off to polish some flowers with the rest of her sisters. A tiny, silvery giggle rang out behind Demon but was quickly cut off as he whipped around, glaring.

"It's not funn . . . ," he said, his voice trailing off as he realized there was nobody there. He scratched his head. *Must have imagined it*, he thought. But the hairs on his neck still prickled as if invisible eyes were watching him.

CHAPTER 5

CANINE CHAOS

He trailed over to Melanie the naiad's spring. She was sitting there, combing her long blue locks with a silver comb.

"Do I really smell bad?" he asked. The unicorn's comment had hurt. Melanie sniffed carefully.

"No more than usual," she said. "But you can have a swim and a wash in my pool if you like. I'll even lend you my new soap if you tell me all about your adventures in Asgard."

Demon eyed her.

"Do you swear not to look while I'm bathing?" he asked.

"Pinkie promise," she said, holding out her little finger.

A little while later, just as he had dried off and got into a clean tunic, he heard the sound of loud barking. Melanie tutted.

"That Golden Dog is so noisy," she said. "I don't know how poor old Amaltheia puts up with him." Golden Dog was a mysterious creature who lived in the Stables with his best friend, the ancient nanny goat who had looked after Zeus when he was little.

Demon cocked his head, listening.

"That's not Golden Dog," he said. "Or at least, it's not only him . . ." Before he could say another word, a whole pack of hounds came racing out of thin air, led by Golden Dog. They were white and very hairy, with their red ears pricked up and long tails that wagged frantically.

"Demon!" they barked, crowding around him and jumping up to put their huge paws on his shoulders. "We found you! We hunted you down! She will be pleased!"

Golden Dog was doing his usual leaping and licking, swiping his long pink tongue over both Demon and Melanie until the naiad screeched.

"Off! Off! Get away from my pool, you wretched beasts!" She grabbed handfuls of waterweed and flung it at the hounds who had leaped into the water and were cavorting around in it like puppies.

Demon hid a smile. Dogs were always so enthusiastic. Then his brain caught up with what he'd just heard.

"Wait!" he said to a particularly playful hound who was licking his clean toes. "Who will be pleased? Did you deliver that note last night?" But the dogs weren't listening to him. They leaped out of the pool, shaking streams of water everywhere, and raced into the Stables. As Demon heard an ominous clatter, he raced after them, but it was too late.

Brooms and buckets lay scattered everywhere. Bion the faun had fallen smack on his face into the poo barrow, and poor Doris the Hydra lay on its back, green legs kicking in the air, with wet paw prints all over it. Before Demon could even open his mouth to shout, he heard a strangled squawk, and the griffin came bounding past, wings flapping, with the whole pack of dogs on its heels.

"Save me, Pan's scrawny kid," it gasped, orange eyes wide with fear.

"STOP!" Demon yelled as he ran after them. "You dogs come back here. Come to heel!" But as the griffin soared into the air, with a leaping hound just missing its lion's tail by a hair, the pack streaked off around Olympus, howling their heads off, and he knew he'd never catch them.

There weren't any animals outside for them to chase, so he turned back to the Stables to survey the damage. Doris was back on its feet, whimpering a little and shaking its nine heads, and Bion had climbed out of the poo barrow and was spitting clumps of straw and other more unmentionable things out of his mouth.

"Are you both all right?" Demon asked.

"I'm fine," Bion said, though he looked a bit pale. Doris just tottered over and nuzzled Demon affectionately.

"More snackies?" it asked hopefully.

Demon caught a flash of yellow out of the corner of his eye as he started to pick things up and set the Stables to rights.

"Come here, Golden," he said sternly. "Who were those hounds, and why did you bring them here? They could have killed poor Griffin and Doris. What were you thinking?"

"Yes, you tell him, young Golden," came a creaky old voice from a nearby stall. "Why, those wretched creatures made such a racket, it nearly turned my milk sour." It was old Amaltheia the nanny goat.

Demon had never seen Golden Dog look so guilty before. The big animal slunk out, tail between his legs and ears back, creeping to Demon's feet on low legs.

"Sorry, Demon," he whined as Demon heard faint nymph and cherub shrieks from outside. "I brought one of them last night to deliver Artemis's message, and he told the others it smelled so good in here that they all wanted to come and fetch you. I didn't think they'd go crazy like that."

Demon felt as if he'd been kicked in the belly by a centaur.

"Wait," he said slowly. "Did you just say that the unicorn message was from ARTEMIS?"

Golden Dog's ears pricked up.

"Yes! Yes!" he barked, wagging his tail. "From Artemis. She wants to see you quite badly. Those hounds are hers."

Demon groaned. The last time he'd seen the

goddess of the hunt, she had threatened to shoot him with her silver bow. Only Hestia the kitchen goddess had been able to stop her. He should have realized at once the hounds were hers.

What on earth could Artemis want with him now? He shivered slightly as he remembered hearing the gossip about poor Actaeon, who'd seen her bathing in a moonlit pool one night by mistake. Artemis had turned him into a white stag and had her hounds hunt him down and tear him to pieces. She was definitely not one of the safer goddesses to tangle with, but if she wanted him, he'd have to go.

"I'd better go and find those hounds," he said.

Demon had never said *it's not my fault* so many times to so many angry nymphs and cherubs. The hounds had left a trail of destruction all around Olympus, knocking off flowers and chasing cherubs up trees.

"It'll take us ages to grow all the blossoms back," said an angry Ophelia, the dryad in charge of the orchards. Finally, Demon tracked the hounds down to the poo chute, where they were licking up the remains of the last barrow load and, even worse, rolling in it. He could hear the hundred-armed monsters below roaring with annoyance.

"Disgusting creatures," he said. "Bad dogs! Come here at once and stop eating that. It'll make you sick."

The largest dog looked up and gave him a doggy grin, smelly smears of brown and green coating its neck.

"But it's so delicious," he barked.

"I don't care," said Demon. "I need to know what this unicorn emergency is and why Artemis wants me."

Immediately, all the hounds sat to attention.

"Artemis! Artemis! Artemis!" they howled, all on

different notes, so it blended together like a song. "Beloved Artemis!"

Demon shook his head. He knew a losing battle when he saw one.

"You're hopeless," he said, walking toward the Stables again. Then he sniffed as a waft of poo-laden air drifted past. "And you smell really bad," he muttered.

When the hounds had stopped howling, Demon returned with Golden Dog, carrying his medicine sack and the magic medicine box.

"Take me to Artemis," he said, clutching Golden's collar as they crowded around him, whacking him with the frantic wagging of their long tails. "Let's see what this unicorn emergency is all about."

As they left, he thought he felt a small hand clutch onto his tunic, but he forgot it almost immediately as he felt the whirling, stomach-churning sensation that meant Golden Dog was taking him through the little gaps in time and space. When it stopped, Demon was in a glade that smelled of pine trees and ancient green things. A shining goddess was standing before him, and Golden Dog had disappeared.

CHAPTER 6

ARTEMIS AWAITS

Artemis was dressed in a knee-length tunic, clasped at the shoulder with a circular silver brooch in the shape of two running stags. In her hand she carried a silver bow, with a quiver of silver arrows slung over her back, and her feet were shod in silver sandals whose ribbons twined up her long legs like growing vines. She smelled of moonlight and violets and fresh blood.

Demon fell to his knees, and then flat on his face, as soon as he saw her. One of those silver-shod feet was tapping angrily on the grass, and she was frowning. This was never a good sign in Demon's experience. A frowning goddess could only lead to one thing. Visions of a large, smoking heap of Demon-shaped charcoal flashed through his head.

"Where have you been, Stable Master?" Artemis asked, and her voice was both loud as the belling of a hundred packs of hounds and soft as a breeze through trees at night. "You have kept me waiting."

"I-I'm s-sorry, Your Moonlight Magnificence," he stammered. "I was away with Hephaestus, there was an emer—" Artemis's foot inserted itself under his jaw, closing his mouth so his words were cut off.

"The smith god's affairs do not concern me," she said, and her tone bit into him as harshly as a giant fire ant. "Only my own. Now get up and face me. I have work for you to do."

As Demon scrambled to his feet, the hounds

crowded around her, rubbing their big hairy heads against her and whining with pleasure as she bent down to pull their long red ears and pat them, speaking to each by name. *Surely a goddess who loves her dogs so much can't be all bad*, he thought.

He looked around at where he was. Tall pine trees soared overhead, their needles soft under his feet. In the sky above, a crescent moon shone among the stars like a shining sliver of cut fingernail. He had just time to wonder if the Pleiades had managed to herd them all back into their right places, when Artemis straightened up from her hounds.

"What do you know about healing unicorns?" she asked abruptly.

Demon thought about lying, but he knew she'd only find him out.

"Not m-much, Your Silvery Serenity," he admitted. "The unicorn on Olympus has never been sick, and

I haven't come across any others." He eyed the goddess cautiously and decided to risk a question. "What's wrong with your one, if you don't mind me asking?"

Artemis frowned again, but this time Demon thought it was with worry.

"It's not just one unicorn, Stable Master. It's my whole herd. All the wild unicorns on earth, in fact. The adult mares are very sick indeed, and some of the foals are near death, though the stallions are fighting it hard." She glared at him, her silver-gray eyes flashing in the dim light. "Can you cure them?"

Demon's heart sank. One sick unicorn was bad enough, but a whole herd? That was going to be almost impossible. He fingered the side of his head where he'd been gored. How was he going to get near them if they felt the same about boys as the one on Olympus did?

"I-I'll do my very best, Your Amazing Archeriness," he said, backing away till he bumped into the rough trunk of a pine tree. "But I'll have to see them first." Artemis took two gliding steps toward him and seized his chin in one long-fingered hand.

"You *will* cure them, Pandemonius," she whispered as softly as moonlight falling on ice. "If only one unicorn dies, I will give you to my hounds to hunt and then let them tear you to pieces one inch at a time. Are you going to fail me?"

Demon thought of poor Actaeon's fate again and shook his head frantically. The hounds crowded around him, all barking together, and he began to tremble. Were they going to eat a bit of him now as a warning not to fail? He squeezed his eyes shut, hoping that maybe it wouldn't hurt too much.

But then something wonderfully unexpected happened. He began to listen to what the hounds were saying.

"We LIKE Demon," they howled.

"He's one of us!"

"We won't eat him!"

Artemis stamped her foot, and the ground trembled.

"YOU WILL IF I SAY SO," she roared. Pine needles showered down around Demon's head like fragrant raindrops. Artemis spoke again, more softly.

"And if you won't, my hounds, I shall encase him in one of these pine trees for all eternity, and let the bears and boars use him for a scratching post." But as Demon began to tremble again, he saw several tall figures step out of the surrounding trees. Literally out of them. These were not dryads or anything like his orchard friend Ophelia up on Olympus. They were green and fierce-looking, and they surrounded the goddess.

"Our pine trees will not take him, Moon Lady, nor will any of the trees of our sisters," said the tallest. "Do not threaten the son of Pan."

"No," said a deep, velvety voice, like mossy bark

on ancient trees. "Do not threaten Pandemonius in my forests, Artemis. I will not allow it." A tall figure with thick, hairy goat legs stepped out from between the trees.

Demon let out a gusty sigh of relief. His dad had arrived!

"Pan!" Artemis spat. "You interfering old goat. I'll do what I like." But Pan shook his curly-bearded head, and his yellow eyes with their slit black pupils narrowed.

"He's a good boy and a good healer," Pan said. "It's time you Olympians showed him some respect. Most of you threaten him and treat him like dirt, but who do you turn to when one of your precious beasts is sick? Has he ever let any of you down?"

Demon's heart swelled, and he felt tears prick at the back of his eyes. His dad had neglected him for most of his life. In fact, he'd never even met the forest god till he came and whisked Demon away to the Stables of the Gods. But it seemed his dad had been noticing things after all. And now he was standing up for him against Zeus's own daughter.

Artemis threw up her hands.

"Oh, very well," she said. "Since you all seem to think so much of the boy, I'll be nice. And anyway, I'm sure he'll cure my unicorns, so none of it will be necessary, anyway."

Pan laughed, striding over to lift Demon up into a god-hug that smelled of pungent green things, goaty musk, and old, stale blood.

"Of course he will," the god chuckled. "Won't you, my boy?"

"Y-yes, Your Dadness," he said breathlessly as his father set him down again. Pan's hugs were always very rib-squeezing.

"All right, then," said Pan. "Now that's settled, I'll be off. I promised your mother I'd drop in on her and the twins, and I'm already late." With that, he disappeared into the trees as if he'd never been there. The dryads slipped back into their pines, and then it was just Demon, Artemis, and the hounds in the glade. Demon had a hollow feeling just below his ribs. For a minute he wished his dad had taken him along. Although he knew his mom was happy with her new babies, he still missed her sometimes.

Then, in the quiet stillness Pan and the dryads had left behind, the hair on the nape of his neck prickled, just as it had back on Olympus. Suddenly, Demon felt a breath on his cheek that shouldn't have been there.

Whirling around, he looked behind him, but there was nobody to be seen.

"No need to be so jumpy, Pandemonius," said Artemis. "I said I'd be nice."

"I-it's not you, Your Moonlight Magnificence," he said. "I just thought . . . well, I just thought someone else was here. But I must have been mistaken."

Artemis laughed. "Maybe there is, maybe there isn't," she said mysteriously. "But come, there is no more time to waste. Bring your things and follow me. My unicorns are waiting."

With a cry like a horn blowing, she ran out of the glade, the hounds loping behind her like white smoke.

CHAPTER 7

GODDESS POWER

Demon had never found it so hard to keep up with someone. As he ran behind the goddess and her hounds, deeper and deeper into the wild, untamed forest, the medicine sack over his shoulder and the magic medicine box under his arm became heavier and heavier.

Suddenly, the magic medicine box lit up and began to flash red.

"Shaking overload," it said in its tinny, metallic voice. "About to initiate emergency travel mode.

High risk of battery drain. Do you want to proceed?"

"Yes," Demon gasped. "Whatever you think is best." What did *high risk of battery drain* even mean, anyway? He had no idea. The box was always talking in silly jargon he couldn't understand.

As the box began to shrink, Demon nearly dropped it. Soon it was so small that he could carry it in the palm of his hand.

"Why have you never done that before?" he panted. "You know my arm nearly falls off with the weight of you every time I have to carry you." But the box didn't reply, so he tucked it into his tunic, beside his precious Pan pipes. *I hope it'll unshrink itself when we get wherever we're going*, he thought. The box had proven temperamental in the past, and he didn't trust it not to let him down again. As he ran on, the worry about how he was going to approach the unicorns raised itself again. What if they wouldn't let him near them? He knew Artemis had promised his dad to be nice, but goddesses were notorious for being fickle. She could still change her mind.

Soon, though, Demon had no room for any thoughts in his head. He was concentrating too hard on putting one running foot in front of the other. His breath came in long, panting gasps, and he had to keep rubbing the sweat out of his eyes with his free hand. The medicine sack in his other hand was beginning to rub a blister onto his shoulder.

"Wait!" he tried to shout, but his throat was too dry. Up ahead, Artemis shouted something out, but he couldn't hear what she said, and it was at that moment that he ran into something. Something that slammed into his middle like a hot, bouncy wire. With an *oof* of pain, he was flung backward onto the ground, completely winded. It was almost a relief to be still, but the feeling didn't last for long. Something dropped onto his stomach from a tree. Something with too many long, hairy legs. Another dropped, and another, onto his head and his legs. He screamed hoarsely as the things began to wrap him in sticky fibers, turning him over and over so fast that he became dizzy.

"Artemis! Help!" he whispered as he heard the hounds baying somewhere away in the distance. But he knew the goddess couldn't hear him. Had she been shouting a warning to him? What was it that had taken him? He tried to stop panicking long enough to look at his captors, but it was hard in the faint moonlight. He could see round bodies, and the glitter of huge, many-faceted eyes, and . . . He squinted. Were those *wings*? He thought of all the creatures he knew, but none of them fitted. Then, quite suddenly, he felt himself being lifted upward.

He tried to struggle, but he was held too tightly in his sticky bonds.

As they soared above the treetops, he turned his head as much as he could. What he saw then made all his limbs freeze solid with fear. He had been taken by what looked like enormous spiders . . . with bat wings! He did love all creatures, but spiders were probably his least favorite. It was just something about the way all those legs scuttled . . .

Over the rush of the wind, he could now hear high, squeaking voices, but he couldn't make out what they were saying. Insect language had never been something he understood easily. What did the spider-bats want with him? Were they going to eat him? He couldn't get a hand free to get at his pipes, and even if he had, putting the spider-bats to sleep while they were all flying through the air didn't seem like such a good plan.

All at once, they were swooping down into the

forest again. Thin pine branches flicked against Demon's face and body, stinging him, but he could do nothing to fend them off.

As the spider-bats laid him on the ground, he struggled again.

"Let me go," he yelled, but the creatures just chittered at him, clicking their legs. Demon shuddered. Why did they have to have so many? He closed his eyes and waited for the biting to start.

But it didn't. Instead, something wet and warm swiped across his forehead.

"Arrgh!" he spluttered, his eyes springing open again.

He was surrounded by hairy white heads, which licked his face mercilessly with long, pink tongues.

"Demon! Demon! Demon!" they barked as the spider-bats soared into the air again.

Now Demon was totally confused—and rather upset.

"Get off me!" he ordered as several pairs of heavy hound paws dug into his chest.

Then Artemis was there, raising a sharp silver arrowhead to slice through his bonds as both the hounds and the spider-bats retreated.

"What just happened?" he demanded when he had scrambled to his feet, too angry to remember his manners. Artemis shrugged, a little smile playing at the corner of her mouth.

"You were being a slowpoke, stumbling along behind me like a tortoise, so I got my little flying friends to give you a ride. What are you complaining about?"

Demon opened his mouth, then closed it again as he saw the steely glint in the goddess's eyes. He knew perfectly well she'd done it on purpose.

"Now," said Artemis, picking sticky bits off her arrow. "You can't go to the unicorns like that. They don't like boys. I'll have to transform you into a girl."

This time Demon's mouth dropped open with shock and stayed that way. Artemis laughed.

"How did you think you were going to enter unicorn lands?" she asked.

Demon found his voice with difficulty.

"I-I don't know, Your Shining Serenity," he said. "I was a bit worried about it, to be honest. But how . . . ? I mean . . ." He gestured down at himself. "I mean, I AM a boy."

Artemis shook her head.

"Not while you're in there," she said, pointing far up ahead to a band of lavender mist across the pathway. Making a doorway with one tiny flick of her hands, she pulled things out of the air faster than Demon's eyes could see. Soon there was a small pile at her feet. Demon could see a long dress, a flowery garland, and some silver jewelry.

"Put them on," she commanded just as a chorus of despairing whinnies of pain drifted out from the mist.

"Oh no," Demon said. "Is that . . . ?" Artemis nodded.

"Yes. The unicorns. We'd better hurry."

Since Demon would do pretty much anything in the world to save a sick beast, he put on his new clothes over his tunic without complaint, though they felt very strange to him. While he was dressing himself, somehow Artemis magicked his hair long and helped him bind it up with the flowery garland and some ribbons. Last of all, she handed him a small flask of golden liquid, which smelled strongly of lily-of-the-valley.

"Rub this all over you. It'll mask the boy scent. And remember—while you're with the unicorns, you will be Pandemonia, not Pandemonius." She turned to the hounds. "You all had better remember it, too!"

Out of the corner of his eye, Demon saw doggy grins all around him, but he didn't care. Being a girl wasn't so hard really, he thought, right up until he tripped over the hem of his long dress and fell flat on his face. Grimacing, he picked himself up, avoiding Artemis's gaze.

"Let's go," he said. "I don't want to keep those poor beasts waiting any longer."

He walked off toward the lavender mist, not waiting for the goddess, hearing the pathetic whinnies grow louder and louder as he got closer. He picked up the skirts of his dress with one hand and began to run, praying his disguise would hold.

"Wait!" Artemis cried out. "You can't go—"

As his foot touched the lavender mist, there was a noise like a thousand silver bells, all ringing at once. Immediately, he was thrown backward, a huge jet of rainbow light slamming into his chest. Flying through the air, he had just time to take one panicked breath before he thudded into the ground at the goddess's feet, scattering the hounds, who fled, howling, with their tails between their legs.

"As I was about to tell you," the goddess said, "you can't enter the mist without me." She reached down and hauled him to his feet.

"Come," she commanded him. "And don't let go of my hand."

CHAPTER 8

UNICORN EMERGENCY

This time as he stepped into it, the pale purple fog curled around him like a cat, winding long tendrils about his body, as if it was learning who and what he was. He clung tightly to Artemis's hand, which was cool and dry, with smooth calluses where she had gripped her bow.

Suddenly, they burst through the misty barrier and out to the other side, followed closely by the hounds.

The unicorn lands were bathed in the faint silver

light of the crescent moon, but Demon had no time to stare around him.

In front of himself and the goddess stood a whole line of unicorn stallions, horns lowered, ready to protect the herd. Their ribs stuck out, and they were quite thin. Behind them, the pathetic whinnying of the mares and foals rose and fell like waves on the sea. Demon's heart squeezed tight with pity.

"Peace," Artemis said. "I bring you a healer."

The biggest stallion trotted forward on shaking legs. Demon could see dark sweat on his silver-white coat.

"But the mist, beloved Goddess," he neighed. "The bells in the mist warned of an intruder!"

"There is no intruder, Moonshadow," Artemis assured him. "Only my maiden, Pandemonia, and myself." She stepped forward and put a hand on his mane. "Let us through. We are here to help you."

Moonshadow shook his head.

"There is no help you can give. The time of the

prophecy is at hand. Only the stars can save us now."

Demon frowned as the goddess tutted impatiently.

"What prophecy?" he asked, making his voice a little higher than normal, since he was supposed to be a girl. The stallion's eyes fell on him. They were the shining blue of a clear summer sky.

"In the time of our foremothers, young maiden," he neighed, "there was a mare called Swifthoof. One day, she was seized by the gift of foretelling. This is what she said: *In the time of the crescent shall come death out of the darkness below. The herd shall know sweetness before pain, and a long sleep with no waking. There is no help unless from the sky stars.*"

He snorted softly.

"None of us knew what it meant. But it has been passed down through the generations, and now it is coming true."

"Well, whatever you believe, Moonshadow, it will do no harm to have Pandemonia look at all of you," said Artemis. The stallion bowed his head.

"Very well, beloved Goddess," he whinnied.

As Demon put his medicine sack down, the line of stallions parted, and he walked forward between their ranks. Behind them, everywhere he could see, there were unicorn bodies littering the ground. Pathetically thin silver-white bodies, with one long white horn the same color as the moonlight in the middle of their foreheads, and smaller, even thinner smoke-gray bodies with stubby horns and manes that stuck up from their tiny curved necks like messy mown grass stalks. Amid the smell of flowers, there was a strong scent of wrongness and rot. The whinnies and groans of pain and despair all around him were heartbreaking.

"Oh no!" Demon whispered. "I think they're all dying."

The goddess stepped in front of Demon, took him by the shoulders, and shook him till his teeth rattled.

"They cannot be allowed to die," she whispered fiercely, her voice frantic. "These are the last wild unicorns left on earth, and if you cannot save them, then goodness and innocence will gradually slip away from the world. This earth needs unicorn magic, or it will turn into a place of war and hatred." She let him go and sank to her knees, weeping, and her tears were like silver rain. Where they fell on the ground, small frail blossoms appeared, their transparent heads drooping as if with grief.

Demon had never seen a goddess cry before, and he didn't know what to do. Clumsily, he bent down and patted Artemis's shoulder.

"I'll do my very best," he whispered. "I don't want them to die, either." Then, picking up his medicine sack again, he approached the nearest unicorn mare.

As he came near, she struggled to her feet, nickering pitifully.

"Shhh!" he said soothingly as she trotted toward him on faltering hooves. "Shhh! I'm ... er ... Pandemonia. I'm here to help."

At first, as she lowered her horn, Demon thought the unicorn was going to gore him. He tensed, ready to run. But she just rested it on his shoulder and leaned her beautiful head into his chest. At least his girl disguise seemed to be holding.

"My baby," she whickered. "Save her!"

Close by, where she had been lying, Demon saw a small body. It was a unicorn foal, and it was so thin that its tiny gray body looked like it was turning to mist. As soon as he touched it, it began to thrash distressingly.

"Hush, little one, hush!" he said, though his own throat was now thick with tears. "I'm not going to hurt you." But the effort seemed to have taken the last strength from the foal, and it went limp under his hand. He could feel the rapid *thump thump* hammering of its tiny heart in its chest, but that was the only sign of life.

Not for the first time, Demon wished Chiron was with him. His old centaur teacher was the wisest and most knowledgeable healer there had ever been, and Demon longed for his advice. Being half a horse himself, surely he would have some idea of how to cure unicorns? But Chiron was miles away on Mount Pelion. Demon would have to manage on his own. He began to examine the foal. But apart from the extreme thinness, he could see nothing wrong with it on the outside.

Suddenly, all around him, unicorns began to scream and thrash, including the stallions who had challenged them. It was a terrible sound, and it made Demon want to throw up from fear and panic. What was wrong with these poor beasts? And how was he ever going to find a cure?

"Do something!" Artemis shouted, and the horror in her voice made the leaves shiver. "Or I swear you will not live to see another dawn!" The hounds around her began to howl.

Demon did the only thing he could. He pulled his dad's magic pipes out of the front of his tunic and blew them.

The screaming was cut off as if with a sharp sword. Every unicorn lay still as death. Every hound lay silent on the ground. Only he and

Artemis were left conscious.

The goddess looked at her hounds, and her eyes were like silver flames as she turned to glare at Demon. Before she could get out a word, Demon waved the pipes at her.

"I'm s-sorry, Your Celestial Shininess," he said quickly. "It was the only way. I'll wake them up again, I promise."

The goddess's eyes narrowed. "Do what you have to, Stable Master. But do it quickly. I do not think there is much time left."

CHAPTER 9

RED FOR DANGER

Demon set to work at once. Many of his patients, like the foal, had gone misty and faint. Using all the skills Chiron had taught him, he examined each unicorn from horn to tail as best he could in the dim light. His flowery garland kept slipping into his eyes, annoying him, but he didn't dare tear it off and stamp on it as he wanted to. It was too risky to take off any part of his girl disguise.

He could still see nothing outwardly wrong with any of the unicorns, and he began to despair of finding anything. He rubbed at his nose absentmindedly. Then he stopped. Yes, the sweet, rotting smell he had noticed before was growing much stronger. Where was it coming from? Kneeling down beside a mare and foal, he closed his eyes and took a long breath.

"Phew!" he gasped, and nearly choked. Bending down, he sniffed at the mare's mouth. Yes, that was where it was coming from!

And then, in a stray beam of moonlight, he saw a trace of red on her silver-white face. Peering closer, and lifting the mare's lip to see inside, he noticed more red smears around her teeth. The smell of sweet rot was overpowering now.

"Surely this must be it," he said, holding his nose.

Just in case, he checked the next unicorn, and the next.

There was only one thing they all had in

common. Every single unicorn had red smears on their teeth. Scraping some off with a wooden spatula, he examined it in the faint moonlight. It definitely wasn't blood. So what was it, then?

"What do unicorns eat?" he muttered to himself. The unicorn in the Stables ate sun hay and ambrosia cake, but what about these wild ones?

Artemis raised her head from where she was sitting among her unconscious hounds, stroking their long ears.

"They get all their nourishment from moon and starlight. I don't know what Chiron has been teaching you. Everyone knows that," she said tartly.

"Well, I didn't," Demon replied, peering once again at the red smears. "I'm a boy, remember? I don't exactly have the most experience with unicorns." Then he suddenly remembered who he was talking to.

"I-I'm sorry, Your Celestial Shininess," he

stammered. "I didn't mean . . ."

"Never mind," said the goddess, her voice impatient. "Get back to work. And don't say you're a you-know-what. They might hear in their sleep."

There was only one thing for it. Demon pulled the magic medicine box out of his tunic and tapped it gently.

"Wake up, box," he said. "I need you." *Please!* he thought. *Please work!*

After a long pause, during which Demon tried not to grit his teeth, the box finally flashed blue.

"Exiting emergency travel mode," it said, making a loud beeping sound. Demon hurriedly set it on the ground as it began to grow. Soon it was its normal size again.

"State nature of ailment," it said.

"Tell me what these red smears are on the unicorn's teeth," Demon said. Immediately, the box's silver lid flipped open, and out whipped a thin bright blue tube with one large sucker on the end. It hovered over the nearest unicorn's mouth, making a slurping noise as it sucked up all the red. Then the tube disappeared back into the box.

"Initiating analysis mode," said the box. A circle of rainbow colors began to whirl on its lid.

"What is that thing?" Artemis asked.

"It's one of Hephaestus's inventions," Demon said. "I don't use it as much as I used to, but it is useful for finding stuff out quickly. It's pretty rude sometimes, but it does come up with answers."

Artemis let out a small huff of laughter, which she quickly stifled.

"That sounds like my brother Hephaestus, all right," she said. "Rude but with answers. How long will it take?"

Demon shook his head.

"I don't kn—" he started to say, but as he was speaking, the rainbow circle stopped, and blue sparks shot out of the box.

"Analysis complete," it said. "Substance is pomegranate."

"Pomegranate?" Demon asked, bewildered.

"I don't understand. Where . . . ?"

"Substance originates from the Underworld," the box said. "Specifically from the palace gardens. No known antidote. Patient will fade away and die shortly. Thank you for your inquiry."

Then it began to beep again—a different, higher beep.

"Battery power drained. Initiating shutdown mode. Solar recharge initiating." With a whirr, its lights went out, and it was silent. Demon tried not to kick it. He knew it would do no good. But now he really was on his own. It was not a comforting feeling.

"Hades!" Artemis snarled suddenly, leaping to her feet. "Persephone!"

Demon whirled around. "Where?" he gasped. Hades was the god of death, and Persephone was his wife. Was she here? Even worse, was *he* here? Demon didn't get along at all with Hades. He had nearly been eaten by Hades's ghost dragons once. But as his eyes flicked everywhere and fear swept over him in a great wave, he saw nobody. He let out a great sigh of relief. And then he remembered.

"Wait," he said slowly. "Hades tricked Persephone with pomegranate seeds, didn't he? And both of them tried to trap me down in the Underworld, too, with pomegranate-seed pastries. But . . . but what have pomegranates got to do with the unicorns?"

"It's the prophecy, stupid bo—I mean, GIRL!" Artemis shouted. "Think about it. *In the time of the crescent shall come death out of the darkness below.* And the *sweetness before pain* must mean the pomegranate. Hades or Persephone are the only ones who could have done this, and I'm going to make them pay!"

Whipping several arrows out of her quiver, the goddess fired them in quick succession at the earth, where they stuck for a moment, silver feathers trembling, and then disappeared downward with a muffled *whoosh*.

"Will those really kill them?" Demon asked. His personal experience of the god of death made him pretty sure that a hundred arrows wouldn't even dent him, let alone just a few. He wasn't sure how tough Persephone was, though.

"Of course not," said Artemis. "It just made me feel better. They'll give them a good sting, however."

Demon was puzzled. It still didn't make any sense.

"But *why* would Hades go after the unicorns?" he asked. "He's got those hell-dragons to pull his chariot, and he must have enough ghosts around to satisfy him. And I know Persephone only cares about her gardens. Orpheus told me so."

"I don't know," she said, her voice grim. "Believe me, though, I will find out. But first, you need to find a cure. That stupid box of yours has to be wrong. There MUST be a way to make my unicorns better."

"The pomegranate is obviously poisoning them," Demon said slowly. "But how? It's only a fruit, really, unless you're down in the Underworld."

Artemis looked at him.

"I really DON'T know what Chiron has been teaching you," she said. "Isn't it obvious?"

It was quite hard to think with a goddess glaring at him as if she wanted to turn him into a beetle. Demon began to pace, his brain whirling. Then he smacked himself in the forehead. It WAS obvious.

"The unicorns are creatures of light," he cried triumphantly. "And those pomegranates come from the Underworld, where it's all dark. No wonder it's poisoning them." Then he frowned.

"It's a pity I don't have any of Hestia's fire left," he said. "That might have helped. But I used it all on Goldbristle the Boar when I was in Asgard."

Artemis raised one thin eyebrow.

"Are you allowed that?" she asked. "Zeus gets very cross if it's taken off Olympus. Why, poor Prometheus . . ."

"I know all about Prometheus having his liver torn out by the Caucasian Eagle every day," Demon interrupted her hastily. "And it's all right. Hestia's fine with me having her fire. I didn't steal it, or anything." He carefully didn't say that Zeus had no idea about his little arrangement with the goddess of the kitchens.

Just then all the unicorns began to thrash and moan again, and one of the hounds let out a whimper.

"Oh no!" he said. "They're waking up."

CHAPTER 10
THE MISSING INGREDIENT

Demon reached frantically for his pipes, putting them to his lips and blowing a short, sharp blast. Immediately, all the beasts slumped back into unconsciousness.

What else did he have that he could use? Since the box was now useless, he began to rummage in his medicine sack.

"Sunflowers," he said. "They're good light medicine. And I think I have some essence of moonflower, too, Maybe a combination of those will do it."

Quickly, he tipped some dried sunflower petals and a little oil into his mortar and ground them up with a few drops of the moonflower essence. When he had finished, he had a sticky gloop that glowed a pale gold.

Gently levering one of the mistiest mare's teeth open with a nearby stick, he tipped a few drops of the mixture in.

Nothing happened, so he tipped in one more.

Still nothing.

"It's not doing anything," he said, feeling despair steal over him like a cloud.

"Then think of something else that will," Artemis growled at him. "And be quick about it. Because the foals are getting worse."

It was true. Some of the foals were now nothing more than a misty outline on the ground.

Demon wanted to howl with frustration. There must be something. What was he missing? Then his eyes fell on the sickle moon, now halfway across the sky. Maybe that was why the unicorns were so thin. Maybe they'd been fighting the pomegranate poison off so hard that they were starving! What had the prophecy said? *There is no help unless from the sky stars.* And what was the moon if not a kind of sky star?

"The moon, Your Silvery Serenity," he said, excitement rising in his voice. "Can you influence the moon?"

Artemis looked at him.

"Of course," she said. "I am a moon goddess, after all. But why?"

Demon spluttered out his theory.

"I need you to make it full," he finished. "I think a proper dose of moonlight will cure them."

"Very well," said Artemis. "But Selene will not be pleased if I meddle for too long. She's in charge of moon matters."

With that, she pulled out an arrow, bigger and brighter than the rest, and attached it to a ball of silver twine she drew from out of thin air. Then she fitted the arrow to the bow, drew it back, and fired.

Immediately, the tethered arrow sped high into the sky, higher and higher until it was no more than a silver spark in the darkness. Then Demon saw the moon tremble as it hit.

Slowly, hand over hand, Artemis drew in the twine. And as she did so, the moon moved. Closer and closer it came to earth, and as it did so, the shadows dropped away from it, revealing more and more of its silvery orb, until it was round and full and fat. Gradually, the night landscape lit up until the unicorns were bathed in a light nearly as bright as day.

One-handed, Artemis tied another arrow to the twine and fired it into a large rock nearby.

"There!" she said. "That should hold it till moonset."

But Demon wasn't looking at her or the moon. He was looking at the unicorns. Already the misty foals were firming up, and the adult unicorns were growing fatter by the second. The moonlight was feeding them.

"Look, Your Moonlight Magnificence!" he said. "It's working!"

"Then wake them up," Artemis said.

Demon blew the wake-up call, and all around him, unicorns began to scramble to their feet. But almost immediately, Demon knew that something was still wrong. A small breeze wafted a delicious scent toward him, and as one, the herd bunched together, totally silent, their horns all facing one way. Then, with a neighing scream, they all charged forward toward a grove of trees that lay a little way off.

"Sweet, sweet, sweet!" they neighed. "Must have more sweet!"

In the moonlight, Demon spotted golden balls hanging from the black-leafed branches. The unicorns shouldered one another out of the way in their eagerness to get at them.

"Oh no!" he yelled, beginning to run. "They're eating pomegranates again!" Pulling his pipes out, he blew again desperately. As if they were cut strings, the unicorns all collapsed together in a heap. But when Demon reached the grove, the sweet smell became overpowering, so delicious that it made his mouth water. He found his hand reaching out toward one of the deadly fruits.

"STOP!" shouted Artemis, grabbing him around the waist and lifting him up. Demon struggled as she dragged him back toward the hounds. As soon as he was away from the smell, she flung him down.

"STAY!" she hissed, and her voice was deadlier than a nest of angry vipers. Striding back toward the grove again, the goddess reached up to the moon, drawing down several of its yellow-white beams into her hands. Shaping them into balls as she went, she began flinging them at the pomegranate trees. As each ball hit a tree, it exploded with a flash of brightness. Soon there were no more trees left, only a deep pit in the ground. But the goddess didn't stop. Pulling down more and more moonbeams, she filled the pit until it was a lake brimming with light.

Stalking back to where Demon lay, she reached down and picked him up by the front of his dress. Her eyes were like silver fire, and he quaked as she looked at him.

"You have failed me, Stable Master," she said in a voice so quiet and menacing that he went still and limp with fear. Her grip tightened. "My unicorns are still not cured. I think I shall give you to my hounds after all. Your father will forgive me. Eventually."

"P-p-please," he gasped. "Give me one more chance, Your B-Bright Beautifulness. I will try again. I WILL cure them this time."

Artemis dropped him disdainfully.

"You have until moonset, Stable Master. I will be back from the Underworld by then. I go to punish my uncle and his wife. If you fail, not only will I give you to my hounds, but I will set my bears on you, too." With that, the goddess dived into the moonlight lake she had created, and disappeared.

Demon stood there for a moment, breathing hard. His heart was crashing around in his chest like one of the fiery bulls on a rampage. He ran his hands through his too-long hair and tried not to panic.

"What shall I use? What shall I use? Think, Demon!" he muttered to himself. Sunflowers and essence of moonflower hadn't worked. But maybe if he added something to them. What else did he have?

Tipping everything out of his medicine sack, he sorted through it frantically.

"Not that, not that, not that," he said. Then something golden caught his eye. It was a ball of fleece from the Golden Ram. *That shines pretty bright*, he thought, setting it aside.

He was just getting up to fetch some of the

silvery flowers that had grown out of Artemis's tears when he felt something brush against his arm, tugging on his dress. Demon turned around. This was getting ridiculous.

"Who ARE you?" he demanded. But there was no reply.

Instead, a small wide-necked bottle half-full of dark dust rolled across the ground toward him, tinkling slightly. The sight of it tickled his memory. It was the stardust he had gathered on the way to send Typhon back to sleep.

"That's it!" he shouted, his voice echoing back at him in the eerie silence. "That's the missing sky star ingredient!"

As if his brain had suddenly added everything up, he now knew exactly what to do. Working fast, he plucked some of the silver tear-flowers and put them in his mortar. After that, he shook in some more sunflower petals and moonflower essence, and flipped in the ball of golden wool. Then he ran over to the moonlight lake and dipped out a measure of what seemed to be liquid light. A little of it slopped onto his fingers, where it fizzed slightly, with a feeling like hot ice.

Carefully, he mixed and pounded everything together, then, last of all, he tipped in half of the stardust. As soon as it hit the surface of the new potion, it began to sparkle. The whole mixture began to bubble, emitting a light so bright that Demon had to squint against it as he carried the mortar carefully over to the heap of fallen unicorns.

One by one, very carefully, he fed a drop into each unicorn's mouth. As soon as it touched the red stains of the pomegranate, they disappeared with a sizzle. By the time he was finished, there was only a scrape of potion left in the bottom of the mortar.

Demon closed his eyes and pulled his pipes out for the fifth time that night. Putting them to his lips and crossing every available finger, and some of his toes, too, he blew a series of trills, hoping against hope for a miracle.

CHAPTER 11

FEAST IN THE FOREST

Almost immediately, he was surrounded by snufflings and tails and happy howls. The hounds had woken and come galumphing toward him on huge paws.

"We're awake, we're awake!" they barked.

As Demon blew one last trill, Moonshadow lifted his head. Then all the unicorns were surrounding him as well, the foals nuzzling him with their soft noses, their little whisks of tails flicking from side to side.

"Are you well?" he asked anxiously,

remembering to pitch his voice a little higher again. He just hoped the flower scent Artemis had made him put on was still holding. He still had to be Pandemonia.

"Never be-he-hetter!" Moonshadow whinnied. "And all thanks to you and our Beloved Goddess!"

"What exactly happened to you?" he asked. The mare who had asked him to save her foal pushed through the crowd of horned heads.

"As far as I remember it," she whinnied, "there was a bang from over there, just before moonrise. It was just as the prophecy said. A big clot of darkness erupted out of the earth, and then we smelled it. The sweetness. It was so delicious that we couldn't resist, but one we'd eaten it, the pain came, and we started to die. I don't really remember anything much after that."

As she finished, Demon noticed a large group of unicorns trotting over to where the things from his medicine sack lay strewn across the ground.

"Don't eat any of that," he cried, but he needn't have worried. The unicorns were neighing in welcome. Demon peered over to see who had come, but there appeared to be nobody there.

He remembered the tug on his dress, and the continual feeling of being watched, which he'd had ever since he returned to Olympus.

"Who is that they're greeting?" he asked the mare casually, holding his breath in anticipation.

"Oh, that's our friend Electra," she whinnied. "I'm surprised you can see her. She's usually invisible."

Suddenly, Demon remembered what Alcyone had said to him in the sun boat.

Electra's invisible . . . she's rather shy . . . I think she might like you!

The seventh of the Pleiades must have followed him!

"Oh, Electra!" he called. "Why don't you come and say hello? I want to say thank you!"

A tiny soft giggle reached him, and then, in the middle of the unicorns, a light began to shine. It revealed a small girl wearing a crown of living stars. As Demon stared, she floated over to him, her feet seeming not to touch the ground.

"You do look funny in a dress," she whispered in his ear. Demon blushed.

"I had to," he whispered back. "It's a disguise." She smiled and reached out to tug his ribbons and adjust his garland, which had slipped over one eye again, just as the moon sank behind the trees.

Almost immediately, Artemis rose from the moonlight lake, trailing moonbeams from her robe. Her face lit up as she saw the unicorns.

"Well, Pandemonia," she said. "I see my hounds and bears will have to go hungry."

"*She* did very well," said Electra, floating over and curtsying to the goddess. "I only had to give *her* the tiniest of hints."

Demon couldn't contain his curiosity any longer.

"What happened in the Underworld, if you don't mind me asking, Your Celestial Shininess?"

Artemis laughed.

"It all turned out to be a big mistake," she said. "Hades and Persephone were having one of their eternal arguments in the garden, and Persephone pulled up all the pomegranate trees in a temper and flung them at him. He threw a darkness bolt at them, and it was so strong that it carried them all the way up here. Of course, because Persephone had touched them, they grew where they fell. They were both very apologetic when they'd finished picking my arrows out of themselves. They both know how important my unicorns are."

Demon tried to imagine arguing with the god of death and failed miserably.

"He . . . er . . . he's not coming up here, is he?" he asked nervously.

"No," said Artemis. "But, come to think of it, he did send you a message."

Demon gulped.

"W-what was it?"

"He said to tell you that the position of keeper to the ghost dragons is still open," the goddess replied.

Demon shuddered. That was *definitely* not a job he wanted.

"I think I'll pass," he said firmly.

"A sensible decision," said Artemis. "And now,

I think that we should have a feast in honor of the unicorns' recovery."

Demon's tummy rumbled loudly. He couldn't remember when he'd last eaten, and he was suddenly VERY hungry.

"What a brilliant idea, Your Amazing Archeriness," he said, grinning. For all her threats, Artemis was pretty nice for a goddess, he thought.

A short while later, six beams of light fell out of the sky. Electra had summoned her sisters to the celebration. Before they sat down to the feast, they poured handfuls of starshine into the new lake, which sparkled with a million rainbow colors in the light of dawn. All the unicorns gathered around to drink, and as they did so, their coats began to glow with health. The last effects of the pomegranate disappeared as if they had never been.

"Why did you follow me?" Demon asked Electra as he tucked into mushroom patties as light as air and little baked chestnuts rolled in honey and crunchy brown sugar. He didn't know where Artemis had conjured the feast from, but he suspected Hestia had had something to do with it.

Electra's shining cheeks turned a little pink.

"Well," she said slowly, "I've always been the curious one of us seven. I like to learn new things—and you're so fascinating with those pipes of yours, and, well . . . I liked you. I don't have many friends, other than my sisters," she said, turning even pinker.

Demon felt his own cheeks mirroring hers.

"Well, you can be my friend if you like," he said. "Only next time, perhaps you might like to let me know you're there. It's a bit hard to be friendly when I can't see you."

"Hey, Demon Boy," Alcyone called over in a

teasing voice. "What are you saying to my sister to make her turn the color of Eos's curtains?"

Her words fell into a sudden deep silence.

"What?" she asked, sounding puzzled, as the unicorns all crowded around, sniffing at Demon suspiciously. "What have I said?"

"Did I hear you ri-hi-hight?" Moonshadow neighed, rearing up. "Is Pandemonia a BOY?"

Artemis held up her hands as his hooves thudded to the ground.

"Yes," she said. "He is."

"You lied to us, Beloved Goddess," he trumpeted. "You broke our rules!"

"Yes I did," said Artemis, rising to face him. "And it was for your own good. Has he done you any harm? No. He has healed you. So what if I disguised him a little?"

Moonshadow's head fell, and he let out a breathy sigh that smelled of moon and stars.

"Very well," he whinnied. "It is true, he has done us a great service. So from now on, while he is in our lands, he shall be an honorary girl, and he shall have the protection and goodwill of all unicorns."

He stamped one hoof.

"Come here, Pandemonia." Demon approached him warily, keeping his eyes on Moonshadow's very long, pointy horn. The stallion kneeled in front of him. "Take my horn, and break off the tip, then take it to our Beloved Goddess."

Demon flinched back.

"Won't that hurt you?" he asked. Moonshadow let out a snort of horsey laughter.

"Not at all," he said. "It will grow back in a trice."

So Demon set his hands on the horn, which felt warm and smooth, like silk over heated honey, and snapped off the very end. Moonshadow was right. It grew back at once. He took it over to Artemis and put it in her hands.

Taking a piece of the silver twine she had used to pull down the moon, she twisted both ends around the broken bit of the horn, winding it around and around so that it hung from a long string. Then she put it over Demon's head, tucking it down into the front of his tunic.

"There," she said. "May the favor of the unicorns be with you always."

"Thank you, Your Celestial Shininess," he said, bowing. "And thank you, Moonshadow."

He stepped backward, tripped over the hem of his dress, and promptly fell over.

"Please can I take this off?" he asked plaintively. "And lose the long hair?"

Artemis and all the Pleiades laughed.

"Certainly not," the goddess said. "Moonshadow has already had enough shocks for one day . . . Pandemonia."

Demon sighed.

He supposed, all things considered, a dress and long hair weren't really that bad. And the garland did smell awfully nice.

He reached for another mushroom patty and turned to Electra.

"So, my invisible friend," he said. "About this being-a-girl stuff. Do you have any handy hints?"

GLOSSARY

PRONUNCIATION GUIDE

THE GREEK GODS

Aphrodite (AF-ruh-DY-tee): Goddess of love and beauty and all things pink and fluffy.

Artemis (AR-te-miss): Goddess of the hunt. Can't decide if she wants to protect animals or kill them.

Chiron (KY-ron): God of the centaurs. Known for his wisdom and healing abilities.

Demeter (duh-MEE-ter): Goddess of plants and the harvest. The original green thumb.

Eos (EE-oss): The Titan goddess of the dawn. Makes things rosy with a simple touch of her fingers.

Hades (HAY-deez): Zeus's brother and the gloomy, fearsome ruler of the Underworld.

Helios (HEE-lee-us): The bright, shiny, and blinding Titan god of the sun.

Hephaestus (hih-FESS-tuss): God of blacksmithing, metalworking, fire, volcanoes, and most things awesome.

Hestia (HESS-tee-ah): Goddess of the hearth and home. Bakes the most heavenly treats.

Morpheus (MOR-fee-us): God of dreams. Brings wonderful (or terrible) visions to the sleeping.

Pan (PAN): God of shepherds and flocks. Frequently found wandering grassy hillsides, playing his pipes.

Persephone (per-SEFF-uh-NEE): Part-time goddess of the Underworld, part-time goddess of spring.

Selene (seh-LEE-NEE): The goddess of the moon.

Zeus (ZOOSS): King of the gods. Fond of smiting people with lightning bolts.

THE NORSE GODS

Frey (FRAY): Shiny, happy god of peace, growth, and sunshine.

Heimdall (HAME-doll): Guardian and herald of Asgard. Has a really loud horn.

Loki (LOW-kee): The sneaky, shape-shifting trickster god of Asgard.

Odin (OH-dinn): The All-Father and ruler of Asgard.

Thor (THOR): Mighty god of thunder who has a giant hammer called Mjolnir (MYAWL-neer).

Thrud (THROOD): Thor's daughter.

OTHER MYTHICAL BEINGS

Amaltheia (ah-mul-THEE-uh): An actual goat who raised Zeus as if he were her own.

Cherubs (CHAIR-ubs): Small flying babies. Mostly cute.

Dryads (DRY-ads): Tree nymphs. Can literally sing trees to life.

Heracles (HAIR-a-kleez): The half-god "hero" who just *loooves* killing magical beasts.

Naiads (NYE-ads): Freshwater nymphs: keeping Olympus clean and refreshed since 500 BC.

Nymphs (NIMFS): Giggly, girly, dancing nature spirits.

Orpheus (OR-fee-us): A musician, a poet, and a real charmer.

Pleiades (PLEE-a-deez): Seven nymph sisters who were transformed into stars back in the day.

> **Maia** (MY-uh): The smallest of the seven nymph sisters.
>
> **Alcyone** (al-SYE-oh-nee): One of the seven nymph sisters.
>
> **Electra** (el-EK-truh): A shy nymph sister. She can become invisible.

Valkyries (VAL-kuh-reez): The shield-maidens who bring fallen heroes to Valhalla.

PLACES

Asgard (ASS-gard): The chilly Northern home of the Norse gods.

Bifrost (BY-frost): A moving rainbow bridge created by Heindall blowing his golden horn.

Mount Pelion (PEEL-ee-un): A mountain on the Aegean Sea where Chiron the centaur lives.

Valhalla (vall-HALL-uh): Official party hall for the heroes and Valkyries.

Yggdrasil (IGG-druh-sill): A giant ash tree that keeps the whole world together.

BEASTS

Centaur (SEN-tor): Half man, half horse, and lucky enough to get the best parts of both.

Colchian Dragon (KOL-kee-un): Guard dragon of Ares, the god of war. Has magical teeth and *supposedly* never sleeps.

Cretan Bull (KREE-tun): A furious, fire-breathing bull. Don't stand too close.

Fafnir (FAVE-neer): A fearsome cursed dragon who guards a stash of gems and gold.

Fenrir (FEN-reer): Mad wolf who has it out for Odin.

Griffin (GRIH-fin): Couldn't decide if it was better to be a lion or an eagle, so decided to be both.

Gullinbursti (GOO-lin-burst-ee): Also known as Goldbristle, he's a glowing golden boar and friend of Frey.

Hydra (HY-druh): Nine-headed water serpent.

Typhon (TY-fon): A terrible two-headed monster.

Unicorns (YU-ne-korns): Horses who managed to sprout a horn from their foreheads. Tend to dislike boys.

Zeus decrees that you . . .

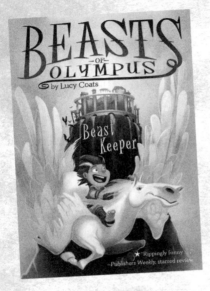

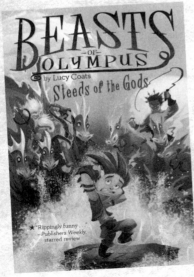

collect all 8 books!

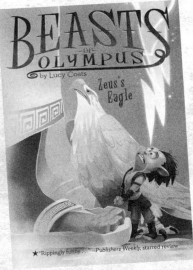

ABOUT THE AUTHOR

Lucy Coats studied English and ancient history at Edinburgh University, then worked in children's publishing, and now writes full-time. She is a gifted children's poet and writes for all ages from two to teenage. She is widely respected for her lively retellings of myths. Her twelve-book series Greek Beasts and Heroes was published by Orion in the UK. Beasts of Olympus is her first US chapter-book series. Lucy's website is www.lucycoats.com. You can also follow her on Twitter @lucycoats.

ABOUT THE ILLUSTRATOR

As a kid, **Brett Bean** made stuff up to get out of trouble. As an adult, Brett makes stuff up to make people happy. Brett creates art for film, TV, games, books, and toys. He works on his tan and artwork in California with his wife, Julie Anne, and son, Finnegan Hobbes. He hopes to leave the world a little bit better for having him. You can find more about Brett and his artwork at www.drawntoitstudios.com.